NODDY™

Noddy Lends a Hand

HarperCollins *Children's Books*

Noddy was very excited as his friend Big-Ears was coming for dinner. Noddy had all the ingredients laid out on his table and he was following the instructions in a cookbook.

But before he got the dinner ready somebody came knock-knock-knocking at Noddy's little front door.

"Noddy! Noddy! Quick, open the door!" It was one of the Skittle children.

"Big-Ears has fallen off his bicycle and hurt his head. The bicycle is smashed to pieces!"

"Quick, tell me where Big-Ears is," said Noddy. "I must help my friend."

"Oh dear, poor Big-Ears" thought Noddy. "I can't bear him to be hurt. I'm coming, Big-Ears, I'm coming."

He soon came to Toy Town Square where the accident had happened. There was Big-Ears, looking rather upset.

"Oh, my dear Noddy," cried Big-Ears. "I feel a bit funny and my dear little bicycle is smashed to bits. Please will you take me home with you?"

Mrs Skittle and Miss Pink Cat helped Big-Ears into Noddy's car. He drove Big-Ears home as fast as he could, but was very careful not to go over any bumps.

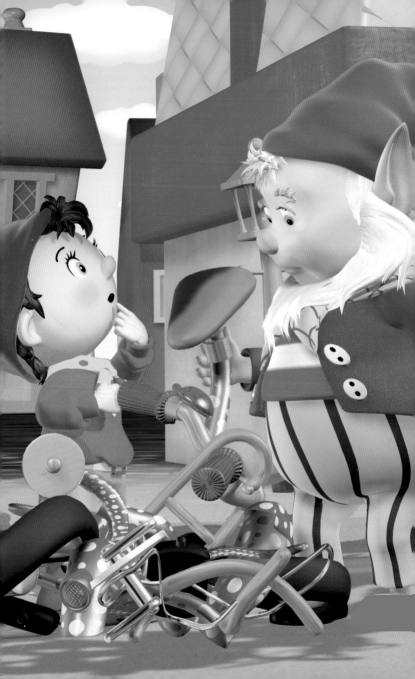

Noddy called the doctor.

"Keep your friend in bed," the doctor said to Noddy. "And don't let him worry, he has had a bad fright. That's very important. HE MUST NOT WORRY. Goodbye, little Noddy."

But Big-Ears worried about everything. He worried about his Toadstool House. Who was going to look after it while Big-Ears stayed with Noddy? So Noddy asked Mrs Skittle and her children to stay in Big-Ears' house for a while to make sure it was safe.

Big-Ears worried about the flowers and plants in his garden.

"You mustn't worry, Big-Ears," Noddy told his friend. "I shall ask Master Tubby Bear to water your garden for you."

This made Big-Ears smile. But as Noddy looked at his friend's face it grew sad again.

"Big-Ears, have you thought of another worry?" Noddy asked.

"I'm sorry, Noddy," said Big-Ears. "It is too big a worry and I don't think even you could fix it. I'm worried about my bicycle!" wept Big-Ears.

"You see, Noddy, it is all smashed to bits and I have no money saved up, so I can't buy a new one. I live so far away, in the woods, that I really must have a bicycle!"

"Don't worry," Noddy told his friend. "I will think of good ideas to raise some money for a new bicycle!"

But it wasn't so easy to think of ideas.

Noddy looked out of the window and saw Clockwork Clown. He was taking the vegetables he had grown to Toy Town to sell them.

"That's it!" thought Noddy, jumping to his feet. "I will grow something and sell it so I will have lots of money to buy Big-Ears a new bicycle." Noddy rushed into Toy Town to find something to grow.

He came to the Ice Cream Parlour and looked in the window.

"Googleberry muffins! Ooooh!" said Noddy. "And toffees. I wish I had some money. I would take some home to Big-Ears."

Then a wonderful idea came into Noddy's head. "I will buy a googleberry muffin and a toffee and plant them to grow googleberry muffin trees and toffee bushes. I will sell them when they are sweet and buy a bicycle for Big-Ears!"

The strange seeds didn't come up the next day or the one after.

Noddy was very sad.

"Perhaps I could make up a song and sell it?" he thought. "Big-Ears says I'm very good at songs. I'll ask people if they would like me to make up a nice song about them."

Master Tubby Bear was delighted at the idea of having a song made up about him and he bought one on the spot. Soon, lots and lots of people wanted Noddy's songs.

One day, Tessie Bear knocked on the door.

"Hello, Noddy," she said. "Dinah Doll will give you a bag of coins if you move all of the presents from her stall to the station so that the train can collect them."

Noddy was very pleased. He leapt in his car and drove straight to Dinah Doll's stall. He gathered all the presents and put them in his car. Then he drove as fast as he could to the station. He was so busy that he didn't notice Martha Monkey giving him a very strange look.

Later that night Mr Plod, Dinah Doll and Martha Monkey knocked on Noddy's door. They all looked very cross indeed.

"Noddy, did you, or did you not, go to Dinah Doll's stall today and steal all the presents that were there?" demanded Mr Plod.

"I did go to Dinah Doll's stall," said Noddy. "But I didn't steal any presents."

"Oh, what a liar," cried Martha Monkey. "I saw him putting the presents in his car!"

"Dinah Doll sent me a message to take the presents to the station for the train to pick up," said Noddy.

"That's right," added Big-Ears. "I heard Tessie Bear give Noddy the message myself."

Mr Plod sent Martha Monkey to fetch Tessie Bear.

Well, of course, Tessie Bear said that she had given Noddy the message. A Goblin had met her in the village and had told her to ask Noddy to fetch the presents.

"Noddy still took those presents," said Mr Plod, "and unless he pays three bags of coins to Dinah Doll he will have to go to jail."

Noddy looked in his piggy bank He had exactly three bags of coins.

Noddy was sad. "That was the money I was saving to buy Big-Ears a new bicycle. What will I do now?"

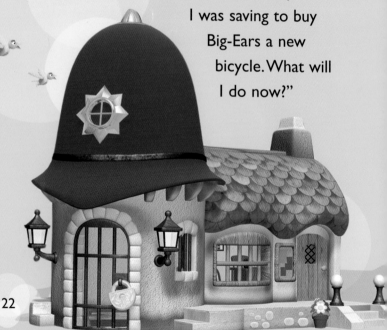

Big-Ears had an idea.

"Noddy! Take your car to the train station and see if you can catch the thief."

Noddy drove to the station. He didn't have to wait very long before the thief appeared. Sly, the Goblin, was trying to put all the presents in a big sack and carry them off.

"Gotcha!" shouted Noddy, jumping out from behind his car.

"Please, Noddy," begged Sly, "don't take me to jail. I'll give you anything you want. Would you like a spell?"

Noddy was very angry with the Goblin, but he knew exactly what he could use the spell for.

Noddy took the Goblin to Big-Ears' broken bicycle.

"If you can mend Big-Ears' bicycle with your spell I won't tell Mr Plod about your trick to steal the presents."

Sly started to sing a very strange song.

Noddy watched as the bicycle began to put itself back together, until it was whole again and just as good as new.

Noddy was so happy that he let Sly go. Then he put the bicycle in the back of his car and drove it home to Big-Ears.

Big-Ears was delighted to have his bicycle back. Noddy had brought him a bunch of balloons to celebrate.

"Everything has come right," said Noddy. "Well - almost everything." He suddenly looked quite sad.

"What hasn't come right?" asked Big-Ears, very concerned.

"Well - I planted a googleberry muffin and a toffee," said Noddy, "and I thought they'd grow into lovely little trees and I could sell them in town. But they didn't grow!"

"You funny little Noddy," laughed Big-Ears. "You are the best friend in the world."